Alphabet Kids Created by **Alle**

# Yang's New Dance

Written by **Dr. Jingyi Hong** and **Patrice Samara**
Illustrated by **Carol Nicklaus** and **Susan Unger**

TOYCHEST
interactive

Meet the Alphabet Kids: Allegra, Elena, Isaac, Oni, Umar and Yang.

They call themselves the Alphabet Kids because that's where they hang out — at the Alphabet Afterschool Center.
Every day they learn something new.

It was playtime at the Alphabet Afterschool Center. "It's time to go out to the playground," said Mrs. Peters.

All the kids ran outside to do different things.
Allegra, Elena and Umar were playing ball.
"Let's see who can kick the ball furthest," said Allegra.

Isaac and Oni were playing on the swings. "Let's see who can swing the highest," said Isaac.

"What is Yang doing?" Oni wondered.

"Let's go see," said Isaac.

Yang was over at one side of the playground with his action figure. Yang's action figure was always with him.

Yang was moving his action figure into different poses, and then doing the same thing himself.

Yang stood up and raised his hands up to the sky. Then he raised his right foot in the air, too.

"Yang, come play kickball with us," said Elena.
"No, not now," said Yang. He kept moving his hands up and down.

"Come play with us, Yang, and let's see how far you can kick the ball," said Isaac and Oni.

Yang continued to move his hands and one foot up and down, copying his action figure. "I am having fun right here," said Yang.

Allegra, Elena, and Umar went back to kicking the ball.

Isaac and Oni were going down the slide. Isaac looked over at Yang and wondered what he was doing.

The next day Yang arrived at the Alphabet Afterschool Center with a man with very gray hair.

Mrs. Peters said, "Yang has brought a special guest to visit us today."

"This is my grandfather," said Yang proudly. "He is visiting from China."

"*Ni hao.* My name is Li Yan Ma," said Yang's grandfather, saying
hello. "You can call me Grandpa Ma. I have come to visit my family
here, and I have a story to tell all of you."

"When I was your age living in China, I lived in a house with a big courtyard. Every day I watched my grandpa and my father practice *Tai Chi*. I will show you some of the moves my father taught me," said Grandpa Ma.

Grandpa Ma crouched down, then gracefully stood up and spread his arms like a big bird ready to fly.

"This position is called 'A White Crane Spreads its Wings.'"

"The crane is a symbol of long life in many Asian countries," said Grandpa Ma.

"Wow! That's so cool!" said Umar.

"Tell us more," said Oni excitedly.

"*Tai Chi* is a very old form of martial arts. People still practice it every day to stay happy and healthy. Shall I do one more pose for you?"

"Yes," everyone said, clapping their hands and jumping up and down.

Grandpa Ma bent his knees and moved his arms as he walked to the left and to the right.

"This position is called 'Floating Clouds.' Your arms move just like clouds in the sky. Would you like to try it?" he asked.

Grandpa Ma asked the kids to line up and leave lots of space around them.

They raised their hands and moved very slowly, exactly following Grandpa Ma.

"Now I understand what Yang and his action figure were doing," said Allegra proudly.

"I can do *Tai Chi*, too," said Isaac, as he moved his arms from side to side.

"Everyone can do *Tai Chi*," smiled Grandpa Ma.

Elena, Oni and Umar also moved round and round and up and down, following Grandpa Ma, Yang, and his action figure.

"Even I can join in!" said Mrs. Peters moving her arms and legs in all directions. Now all the Alphabet Kids can have fun doing Yang's New Dance.

"*Zai jian* – goodbye," said Grandpa Ma. The Alphabet Kids will always remember him and his *Tai Chi* lessons.